F.A. BERR

MEDIA CENTER

Bethel, CT 06801

FIND MY BLANKET

by Susan Brady

J. B. Lippincott · New York

Find My Blanket
Copyright © 1988 by Susan Brady
Printed in the U.S.A. All rights reserved.
10 9 8 7 6 5 4 3 2 1
First Edition

Library of Congress Cataloging-in-Publication Data
Brady, Susan.
Find my blanket.

   Summary: Sam Mouse hates to miss all the fun when
he goes to bed before all his older brothers and
sisters, so he hides his favorite blanket and asks
them to help him find it.
   [1. Mice—Fiction. 2. Brothers and sisters—
Fiction. 3. Bedtime—Fiction. 4. Blankets—Fiction]
I. Title.
PZ7.B72974Fi 1988   [E]   87-45310
ISBN 0-397-32247-X
ISBN 0-397-32248-8 (lib. bdg.)

Sam liked to snuggle with his little blanket in his warm bed at night. Everyone knew he could not sleep without it.

But he did not like to miss all the fun his sisters and brothers had after he went to sleep.

So one night he had an idea.

First he called to his brother Paul.
"What do you want?" asked Paul.
"I lost my blanket. Will you help me look for it?"
asked Sam. "I can't go to sleep without my blanket."
"I'll find it," said Paul.

Paul looked under the bed. The blanket was not
there, but he found a boat.

Then Paul looked under the pillow. The blanket
was not there, but he found crayons.

"I thought you went to bed," said Sam's sister Emily.

"I lost my blanket," said Sam. "I can't sleep without it."

"I'll find it," said Emily.
So she looked for the blanket behind the door and
in the toy box and under Lion and behind Bear.
She did not find the blanket in any of those places,
but she found a ball.

"What are you doing?" asked Sam's brother Harry. "We're looking for Sam's blanket," said Emily, and she looked through the drawers. The blanket was not there, but she found a box of shells.

"I'll find it," said Harry, and he looked inside the
closet. He found Sam's cup, but not the blanket.

"What are you playing?" asked Sam's sister Becky.
"We're not playing. I lost my blanket," said Sam.
"I can't sleep without it."
"I'll find it!" cried Becky.

Becky looked under the slide.

The blanket was not there.

"What are you doing?" asked Sam's mother.
"We've been looking and looking for Sam's
blanket, but we can't find it anywhere," said Becky.

"It's too bad we can't find your blanket, Sam. With
all this looking, we may not have time for cocoa
and toast before bed!" said his mother.

"Cocoa and toast!"

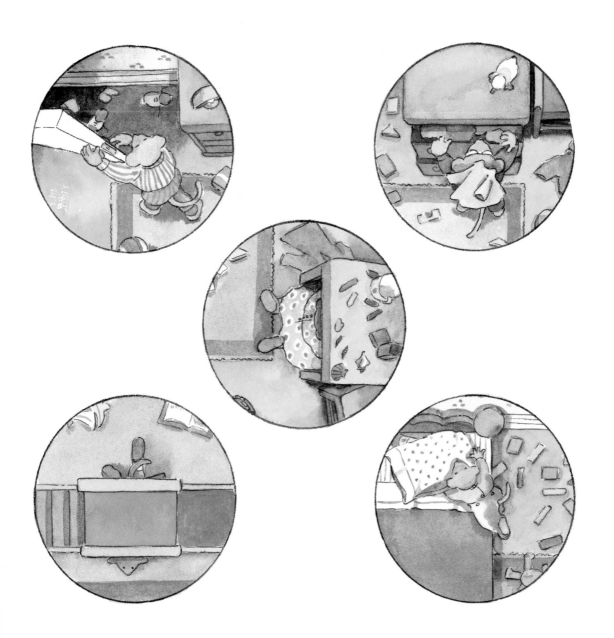

"Look! I found my blanket," called Sam.
"I'm so glad!" said his mother. "Now we can have our cocoa and toast."

Afterward, everyone helped clean up Sam's room.

Then Sam went to bed. He liked to snuggle with his little blanket in his warm bed at night.
Good night, Sam.

E
BRA

Brady, Susan

Find my blanket

DATE DUE

OCT 27			
Matteo			
NOV 13			

Demco, Inc 38-293